Lure Of The Deep
By Chelsea Allen

Library of Congress Control Number: pending

Any references to historical events, real people, or real places are used fictitiously. Names, characters, and places are products of the author's imagination.

Front cover design by Jaded by Design

Printed in the United States of America.

First printing edition 2022.

www.chelseaallenauthor.com

Chapter One

The waves were high as they crashed against the side of the ship, rocking it back and forth across the Dark Sea. The smell of salt water filled the air as the wind whipped across Erin's face. Navigating the storm was of the essence to make it to the port of Tortuga where the crew could unload and refresh for a few days after being out at sea for months on end. The ship creaked and groaned as the waves continued to crash onboard, tossing around anything not tied down. The crew worked tirelessly as the captain continued to fight through the hurricane tearing the ocean apart. This was the biggest storm they had seen in years and they were in the heart of it, with little hope of surviving. The helm became hard to hold as Erin yelled in frustration, gripping it tightly with both hands, with all the strength she could muster.

"Just a little longer maties, we're almost through!" Erin exclaimed to her crew below as the wind continued to billow all around them.

The waves continued to carry the ship across the Dark Sea as the wind filled the sail. It felt like hours they had been battling the storm when finally, The Hollow caught a break. As the ship rocked along the sea, the storm started to part. Erin peered through the spyglass and could see the faint glow of Tortuga through the thick fog.

"Land ho!" Erin yelled, thankful that they had survived the storm's brutality and were just a few miles from making shore at the port.

Though the sea was turbulent and the wind was fierce, a calm radiated throughout the crew, knowing they weren't going to die this night. Erin continued to navigate the Dark Sea to Tortuga and commanded the anchor to be released. As the ship docked right off the port, the crew made their way off the ship and onto the dock. Finally, they were on dry land. The dim lanterns of the island lit the way for the crew to make their way to the brothel. Erin was the last one off the ship, after all, it was her baby and the captain always sees the crew off. They were the closest thing to a family that she had.

The street was filled with people, laughing, and stumbling around. A group of drunk men was singing a familiar sea shanty nearby, as the local whores were looking for their nightly customers. Erin jumped down from the ship and landed on the dock with a forceful 'thud.' Her leather pirate boots glistened with rain as she made her way off the dock and onto the island. With her left hand, she put her tricorne hat atop her head, smoothing her long fire red hair down the sides, curling naturally from the rain as her vivid green eyes sparkled in the moonlight.

As Erin walked across the island to the nearest tavern, the sounds of various conversations filled the air. The

Crying Maiden was brightly lit from the inside, with a bar downstairs and the brothel upstairs. She entered through the door and sat down at an empty table near the back, people watching and listening to the arguments and flirtation that bustled all around her.

"What can I getcha miss?" Bronn asked.

"Grog please, sir," Erin replied.

A few moments later, Bronn returned with a cup full of grog. He smiled at her then placed it in front of Erin and walked away back to the bar. Erin took a sip and put the cup back down, keeping her hands wrapped around it for comfort. The air smelled stale, a mix of sex and rum as the lanterns scattered throughout the tavern burned bright. She looked over and saw a scantily dressed woman leading a man up the stairs, no doubt to have her way with him and earn a few doubloons The tavern grew louder the later it got, but Erin didn't hear anything. She was tuned out in her little world.

Just then a ruckus came from outside the tavern and a man came flying through the door, landing on his back on the floor. He scrambled to get to his feet quickly and ran for cover behind the bar.

"Oi is anyone else going to challenge me tonight!" a man shouted, as he busted through the door. The tavern grew quiet and still, no one dared to move a muscle.

"Well don't just stare you maggots, fetch me some rum!" He shouted to the men following behind him.

They scattered throughout the bar, several fetched rum while others grabbed the ladies and forced themselves upon them. The stench of fish wafted off the men throughout the tavern as the one in charge took a seat at the table next to Erin's. He had a long, thick black beard on his face and his eyes were sunken in from age and endless sun exposure no doubt and he too wore a tricorne hat with the jolly roger embroidered upon it. It only took Erin a second to recognize him for tales of this man were legendary, Captain Blackstone.

Erin watched as he hobbled his way over to the table next to hers, taking a seat. A man returned with a bottle of rum and handed it to Blackstone carefully, as he proceeded to slowly back away. The terror on his face was clear as day as he walked back to the bar and helped Bronn clean the bar top. Blackstone was a legend amongst pirates; taking whatever he wanted and never suffering the consequences. Anyone who dared confront him would be forced to walk the plank.

Erin knew if she and her crew were to make it out of Tortuga alive, they'd have to avoid Blackstone at all costs. She was on a mission, one surely to pique the interest of the world's most legendary pirate. If word got out about where she was headed, war would ensue and Erin was not going to risk losing everything because of one greedy pirate.

As the night carried on, Erin watched Blackstone carefully, studying him and his interactions with his men. She must have watched him for hours as they drank and frolicked about. Finally, he stood up from the table and made his way across the tavern to a woman with blonde hair who'd been flirting with him all night. From a distance, Erin could see the wench run a finger across his chest and whisper something in his ear before he followed her up the stairs to the waiting bedroom for the night.

"Avast ye, I am retiring for the evening you scallywags!" Blackstone announced.

A cheer erupted throughout the tavern as men lifted their cups of grog in the air to salute the captain on his conquest for the evening.

Erin looked around and noticed the noise of the tavern was dying down the later into the evening it got. That's when she noticed him staring at her from across the room. He had short, shaggy black hair and piercing blue eyes that seemed to peer right into her soul. His olive skin was tanned from the sun while his muscles bulged from under his shirt.

Erin looked down at the table, trying to avoid further eye contact with the mysterious man. She reached into her satchel and pulled out a bunch of rolled-up maps, unrolling them onto the table. Erin studied one map in particular, it was hand-drawn, comparing it to the much larger standard map on the side. She traced several routes with her finger and then would draw them on the other. As Erin dipped her quill into the ink, a shadow loomed over her, blocking out the light, making it impossible to see the map any longer.

Erin looked up and saw the mysterious man who was staring at her standing by her table.

"Mind if I sit with ye, lass?" The man asked.

"Yes, I do mind. I'm busy," She retorted harshly.

The man proceeded to pull out a chair and take a seat across from Erin, looking at the maps all over the table.

"What are you drawing?" He asked.

"It's nothing," Erin lied as she set the quill down and started to roll the maps back up, sticking them into her satchel.

"I'm not interested, so please go away," Erin said.

"Women generally fight over me, not turn me away," The man said smugly.

"Well, I'm not most women," Erin sneered.

"I like that about you, lass. What's your name?" He asked.

"None of your business," Erin snapped as she stood up from the table, swinging the satchel over her head and onto her shoulder.

"You've got fire in you. I'm Dean," He said.

"You don't take no for an answer, do you, Dean?" She asked smugly.

Dean simply smiled and chuckled at her question as he stood up from the table and proceeded to walk away from Erin. Relieved, she sat back down and quickly finished her grog. Female pirates were far and few between, so Erin had a way of turning heads whenever she made port, always attracting the attention of lonely men. However, she never reciprocated their advances, mostly because of her grim past that haunted her every night.

Erin grew up as an orphan, being passed around from one orphanage to another until she turned fifteen. It was then that Erin ran away and stole the doubloons off a drunk and used the coins to purchase The Hollow. She then found a crew of like-minded misfits to sail with her, always keeping to the sea, looking for their next adventure.

Erin learned quickly at a young age that you can't trust anyone and that there was no such thing as love or family. After she was abandoned as a baby, she grew up alone, never able to find a stable home. Instead, she had to live in the squalor of the orphanages with hundreds of other children, always fighting for attention and acceptance that never came. Erin took matters into her own hands, creating the life she wanted, rather than the life she was born into.

She was a fierce little thing, sure of herself as she radiated confidence many only wished they had. She knew that in life, the only person you could depend on was yourself. If you wanted something, you got it for yourself; no one was going to hand you anything, especially for free. But Erin wasn't looking for a handout, instead what she desired was only something that could be found on an uncharted island off the coast of the Atlantic Ocean called the Island of the Immortals.

For weeks, Erin had been having the same dream over and over that contained the coordinates of the lost island. The mysterious island was rumored to have an Elixir of Immortality which had long been a legend among the pirate community for centuries, however, it had never been found. Rumors circulated about the dangers that one might encounter on the way to the island, along with the gruesome and terrifying stories of the inhabitants that once lived there.

Erin never believed in the existence of the island or the elixir until the dream started haunting her night after night. Once the location was revealed to her, she knew she had to go after it. With the crew behind her and The Hollow in ship shape, she knew they could find the mysterious island and claim the elixir for themselves.

Erin looked over at the bar and held her cup up in the air, signaling to Bronn that she needed a refill. He filled another cup with grog and walked it over to her, handing it to her carefully, taking in her beauty before he smiled and walked away. Erin didn't notice that he was checking her out, she was only focused on one thing; finding the elixir.

Erin grabbed the hand-drawn map out of the satchel and unrolled it back onto the table. She studied it carefully, looking at the various routes she could take to the mysterious island, but every route was plagued by some sort of rumored danger. The first route took her through Pirates Bay, where the sea hag was said to inhabit. While the second route took her straight through Devil's Cavern, where the legend of the Kraken was said to have sent hundreds of sailors to their deaths. It was the third route that Erin considered, the route that would take them through Widow's Crossing, where the sirens were rumored to exist.

According to the legends, sirens were dark mermaid-like creatures, cursed to haunt the sea for eternity. Anyone that dared to cross their path, was never seen or heard from again. Davey Jones' Locker was littered with sunken ships and the bodies of men that tried to sail through Widow's Crossing and encountered the sirens. They say that as you enter their territory, you'll hear beautiful and melodic music fill the air. It intoxicates you, leading you to take your own life. The ones who aren't affected by the haunting melody, go down with the ship, as no one has ever successfully sailed through the crossing and returned to tell the tale.

Erin didn't believe the legends. The Kraken, The Sea Hag, and The Sirens were just stories you tell children to get them to behave. Erin traced the three routes with her fingers, estimating the distance between them when she finally decided to take the route through Widow's Crossing. It was shorter, maybe 4 or 5 days at sea, tops, compared to the other options.

Erin drew the path from Tortuga to a dot she made in the middle of the Atlantic Ocean where the island was located. Now that she had it all mapped out, she was ready to set sail, however, she knew there was going to be no rounding up her crew at this late hour so instead she rolled up the map, placed it in her satchel, and stood up from the table, walking over to Bronn behind the bar.

"How much for a room for the evening, sir?" She asked him.

"It's 5 doubloons lass, but are ye sure ye want to stay here?" He asked confused.

Erin considered trying to locate the nearest inn but as a wave of exhaustion finally hit her, she simply nodded her head in reply, handing Bronn 5 gold doubloons from her pocket.

"Upstairs, last door on the left," He said.

"No one should bother ye in there tonight," He added.

Erin thanked him and turned to head to the stairs at the back of the tavern when she turned to see Dean standing right in front of her, blocking her path.

"Staying the night are ya, lass?" He asked.

Erin ignored his question and stepped out to the right to go around him. Dean stepped back in front of her again, unwilling to let her pass.

"Let me by!" Erin exclaimed.

"Not until you agree to take me with you to the Island of the...."

"Shhh," Erin whispered as she grabbed him by the arm and pulled him to the side.

"How do you know where I'm going?" She asked him.

"I recognize the map you drew. It's the same one I saw in my dream," He replied.

"Your dream?" She asked confused.

"You know what I'm talking about," He said.

"I won't let you leave here without me unless you want me to announce to everyone in the tavern of your journey," Dean threatened.

Exhausted and frustrated, Erin let out a deep sigh.

"Alright, you can join me and my crew but don't think you're getting free passage," She said.

"I knew you'd say that. Here ye are," He replied, handing her a small leather purse filled with gold doubloons.

"How did you…" Erin started to ask but then she thought better of it and grabbed the money instead.

She knew there was more than met the eye with Dean and several unanswered questions raced through her mind, but she would get to the bottom of it tomorrow. Tonight, she needed to rest.

"Meet me here in the morning when the sun meets the horizon," Erin said as she stepped around Dean and headed towards the stairs.

"I'll be here, lass," He called behind her, a wide handsome smile upon his face.

Erin simply kept walking and refused to turn back to look at him. She ascended the stairs, one by one, until finally she made it to the top and turned down the hall, walking to the last door on the left. She opened the door and stepped inside, locking the door with the key that was already in the lock.

The room was small, as was the bed, but it was only for one night. The dim light from the lantern did little to accentuate the room. Wallpaper was peeling from the walls and stains covered the wood floor. Erin tried not to think about the things that happened in this room and had just hoped that at least the sheets were clean.

She took her tricorne hat off the top of her head and set it down on the table next to the bed. Next, she pulled off her leather boots, tossing them on the floor with a 'thud' as she laid down on the tiny bed, waiting for sleep to overtake her.

The jungle was thick with brush and trees with the air so humid that you could choke on it. Birds chirped off in the distance as the sound of the waves crashing on the beach made the entire place feel very serene. The moonlight was so bright, illuminating everything in its wake. Erin walked along the beach watching the crustaceans dig in the sand as the water washed seashells up onto her boots.

Just then a melodic tune filled the salty air, mesmerizing Erin where she stood. She stopped walking and looked around, searching for the source of the music but she couldn't find anything or anyone. She was alone.

Erin turned in the direction of the beautiful melody and followed it into the jungle, walking carefully to not trip on the branches that littered the jungle floor. She followed the music for what felt like miles, deeper and deeper into the jungle until the jungle canopy was so thick, that even the moonlight couldn't penetrate it.

"Erin...come here Erin," a harmonious voice whispered.

Erin jumped and franticly looked around, but there was nothing. Just her and the trees. Then the mysterious voice came again.

"Erin...just a little further," the voice said.

The voice was so hauntingly beautiful that she didn't fear it. Instead, she was intrigued. She moved forward through the brush, pushing branches out of her way as she made her way through the dense jungle following the voice. Just then, something grabbed Erin's leg and pulled her down onto the ground, dragging her backward. Erin screamed and tried to dig her nails into the dirt, grasping for any vines or tree trunks she could reach, but it was no use. Whatever had her was strong and it wasn't going to let her go.

Erin woke up and shot straight up in bed, unable to catch her breath. She clutched her chest and tried to control her breathing when she noticed a pain in her fingertips. She looked down at her nails to see they were covered in dried blood and her fingertips were bruised purple. She flashed back to her dream where she was drug through the jungle and her heart started to race.

Just then a knock sounded at the door, making Erin jump out of her skin.

"Open up lass!" Dean shouted through the door.

It was Dean. As much as she disliked him, she was oddly comforted by the fact that it was him at the door and that she wasn't alone any longer.

Erin couldn't figure out how she had the same injuries that she sustained in her dream, but there was no time to question it. The sun was rising off the horizon and it was time to set sail. She climbed out of bed and pulled on her boots, grabbing her tricorne hat off the table as she headed towards the door.

Erin unlocked the door and pulled it open to see Dean smiling that devilish grin at her.

"Sleep well?" He asked.

"Yeah, great actually," Erin lied, hiding her hands from his view.

"Then let's gather ye crew and get going," He said.

"Just remember, I'm the captain, so you play by my rules," She replied.

Dean laughed and grinned even wider.

"Yes ma'am," He chuckled.

Erin rolled her eyes and pushed past him, leading the way down the hallway to the stairs. They descended each step quietly until they reached the main floor. Men were scattered throughout the tavern, most of them passed out on the floor or tables. Others were playing cards and still drinking all the rum they could get their hands on.

Erin and Dean headed out of the tavern and onto the street. She looked around for her crew, not knowing where they got off to the night before when she heard snoring come from an empty pig pen next to the tavern. It was no surprise as she peeked over the fencing and saw her crew, sprawled out on the muddy ground. They always had a habit of sleeping in animal pens after they drank too much. Erin chuckled to herself as she looked around for something to wake them with when she saw a pail full of water to her right. She grabbed the pail and threw the water on the men, watching them shoot straight up to a sitting position, confused and hungover.

"Oi, what be the meanin' of this?" Malakai asked, still half asleep.

"Avast ye maties, it's time to hoist the sail and raise the anchor, we've got an island to find!" Erin exclaimed.

"Aye Aye captain," The crew answered in unison.

As the crew stood one by one, they followed her off the island towards the dock to the waiting ship.

"This is your ship?" Dean asked as they approached The Hollow.

"It is, had her for ten years," Erin replied proudly.

"Who'd ye steal it from?" Dean chuckled.

"Just climb aboard," Erin said, annoyed.

Dean, Erin, and the crew all climbed onto The Hollow, scattering to their respective locations throughout the ship. Dean of course followed Erin to the helm and took a seat on an empty crate, watching her, studying her.

"Raise the anchor!" Erin commanded.

As the crew followed her order, the ship jerked forward out onto the briny deep, leaving Tortuga behind.

Chapter Two

It had been hours since they left Tortuga. A warm breeze was blowing and the sea was silent. The sun illuminated the clear sky as it shone brightly down upon The Hollow. Erin was manning the helm, keeping an eye out for any danger that they may encounter. Dean was still sitting on the crate as he studied the maps that Erin obtained.

"You drew this from your dream?" Dean asked.

"Yes, it kept coming to me night after night and wouldn't stop until I traced it out," Erin replied.

"How could we have had the same dream?" Dean asked.

"How do we know it's the same?" Erin asked.

"Good point, lass," Dean replied, straightening up to tell his tale.

"Night after night the same dream would come to me, just like it had for you. I would be walking through the jungle, the air so thick from the heat you could barely breathe. A voice would suddenly call out my name so mesmerizingly that I'd follow it deeper into the jungle to a mysterious cave. But one night the dream was different, it was violent and aggressive. I was attacked by this horde of crows as they dove through the air and headed straight for me. They pecked at me, leaving bloody scratches all over my body. I screamed out for them to stop and once I did, they exploded into a black mist that transformed into a man with red eyes and markings all over his skin. The man said to 'run' as he burst back into a black mist and dissipated into the air. That's when I would wake up and have the coordinates in my head," Dean said.

"What do you think it means?" Dean asked.

"I don't know. I thought I was the only one who knew about the island, but yet, here you are," She replied harshly.

"You don't like me much," Dean chuckled.

"Was that a question?" Erin asked.

"More of an observation, lass," Dean replied.

Erin stayed silent for several moments, trying to collect her thoughts when finally, she responded to Dean.

"Why are you interested in the elixir?"

"You waste no time I see," Dean said.

"I just want to understand your motives," Erin replied.

Dean sucked in a deep breath and exhaled slowly out of his mouth.

"If you must know, I'm not after the elixir. I'm going to the island to die," Dean said sadly.

"To die? Why would you want to die?" Erin asked him confused.

"Because I deserve to die. I'm the reason my wife and daughter passed away and I don't deserve to live in a world where they no longer exist," Dean said.

Erin felt an ache deep in her chest. This was the most vulnerable Dean had been since they met and she couldn't help but feel for him and understand the pain he was in.

"How did they die?" Erin asked calmly.

"I was at sea and had left them behind because I thought it was too dangerous for them to join me. They ended up succumbing to the plague that tore through our town," Dean replied.

"I came back to find them buried in a mass grave," He added.

"I'm sorry for your loss but they would want you to live your life, Dean. It wasn't your fault. Things happen beyond our control," Erin replied.

"I just want to know they're at peace," Dean said as tears welled in his eyes.

Erin took her hand and wiped away the tears that were falling from Dean's eyes. She really liked his honesty and vulnerability. Dean reached up and grabbed Erin's hand holding it for a few seconds before she pulled away.

"We should get back to the maps," Erin stated, trying to change the subject.

"You don't like to get personal, do you?" Dean asked her.

"I don't trust anyone. I keep to myself and my crew. They're the only family I've ever known," Erin said honestly.

Feeling a sadness radiate through her body, Erin realized that was the first time she ever admitted that out loud to anyone. She always considered the crew her friends but to call them family, meant something different, something deeper than Erin was willing to admit to herself at that moment.

Her green eyes echoed a sadness that filled her body from head to toe.

"Don't be sad lass, having people to depend on is everything. You're not as alone as you think," Dean said.

Erin considered his words and realized he was right. Erin hadn't been alone in years; she had her crew of misfits and they always protected Erin at any cost. They were her brothers and all the family she'd ever need.

"I just grew up so alone, bouncing from one orphanage to another, never knowing what family was or truly meant. But you're right, I'm not alone, my crew is everything to me," Erin said.

"Then why do you want the elixir?" Dean asked.

"I don't know… I always thought to live forever was the ultimate desire. Always sailing from one adventure to the next, defying death; what could be better?" Erin replied.

"Death is what keeps us living. The fear of dying is what fuels our actions and ability to love. Without that fear, nothing is worth living for," Dean said.

"We'd just be going through the motions," He added.

Erin paused for a few moments, turning Dean's words over in her mind.

"But you're afraid to live yourself…" Erin stated.

Dean looked deep into her vivid green eyes and said, "Then I guess I should practice what I preach."

Erin smiled at Dean, as he took her hand again, only this time, Erin didn't pull away. He held her hand for what felt like an eternity as Erin sat down next to him on the crate as they conversed with one another.

"Tell me about your family," Erin said.

"Sarah was beautiful, smart, and strong. I knew her since we were children, our mothers were best friends. I came from a high-born family in Crystal Bay, where every want and desire was satiated but it wasn't what I wanted. I wasn't happy and when I told Sarah of my feelings, she reciprocated them. Together we ran away with nothing to our names but love and trust. We eventually made it to a town called Hollow Point and you'd think the name would be enough to make us turn back, but we decided to build a life there instead. Sarah became pregnant with Annie as I went to work on the docks. It was a simple life and everything we ever dreamed of. Then one day, the fishermen asked me to assist them at sea since one of their men had taken ill. I accepted the invitation as it was for only a fortnight thinking that Sarah and Annie would be alright at home as the rough sea was no place for them to be," Dean replied, taking a moment to catch his breath.

"I thought they would be safe at home. After all, nothing ever happened in Hollow Point so I left with the crew, leaving Annie and Sarah at home. When we returned, we found the town decimated. Homes and buildings burned to the ground, mass graves of bodies everywhere. The stench alone made your stomach turn. I ran from the docks to my home, which was a little more than a mile away and the house was empty, only a red X adorned the front door. I searched high and low for Sarah and Annie for hours when finally, the local priest stopped me and told me where to find them. I ran so fast thinking I'd find them alive only to arrive at a mass grave of rotting bodies. My family was gone and it was all my fault. I should have taken them with me or declined the offer, but instead, I left them to die alone," Dean said.

Erin rubbed Dean's back as she said, "There's nothing you could have done differently. Their fate was sealed and yours would've been too if you had stayed. No one is immune to the diseases of the time Dean and it strikes without warning. Sarah and Annie knew how much you loved them, that's all that matters."

Dean mulled over Erin's words. She was right. They were either going to die at sea or of the plague, but either way their fate was sealed and Dean couldn't change that.

"Tell me about the legend of the island," Dean said.

"It's a long story," Erin said.

"I've got time," Dean replied with a smile.

"Well, they say that the island was once a thriving and magical place inhabited by immortal Indigenous people. They called themselves The Crow Men because they had magical abilities where they could transform into the creature at will. Crows are said to be intelligent and cunning animals, able to learn and adapt to their environment and to the enemies of The Crow Men, the creature was an omen of their impending death," Erin said.

"The Crow Men were a kind and majestic people who protected their land and gave tribute to their gods, caring for the land and the sacred gift of immortality they had been given. One night, a captain found himself adrift at sea after his ship was taken down by the Kraken. He made his way to the island where The Crow Men took pity on the man and welcomed him into their home. It would be the greatest mistake The Crow Men would ever make because that very sea captain was something unnatural, something dark. The next morning when they awoke, they found all their women raped with their throats slashed and their bodies littered throughout the island. The Crow Men took revenge on the sea captain and flayed him alive, going against their very nature, unleashing an evil curse upon the island. The beauty and peace of the island died out becoming dark and uninhabitable as did The Crow Men. Their gift of immortality was revoked, nevermore to continue their ancestral line," Erin continued.

"The curse trapped the murderous captain's spirit on the island so he would forever have to live with the pain of his victims, never to move on or find peace. From that day forward, the island was deemed evil and was lost to the times, never again appearing on any maps. Anyone that dared to search for the lost island never lived to tell the tale," Erin added.

"If no one has ever lived to tell the tale, then how do we know these Crow Men existed? It sounds like an old wives tale to me," Dean said.

Erin chuckled and looked at Dean.

"Then we shouldn't have a problem accessing the island," Erin said, pausing for a moment to mull over her thoughts.

"What about the elixir?" Dean asked.

"It's said that the elixir grants immortality only to the one that is deemed worthy, but it comes at a steep price," Erin replied.

"If the elixir comes at a steep price, then why would you want it for yourself and ye crew without knowing the consequences?" Dean asked Erin.

"It seems to me that you have so much to live for and this island only contains pain and death," Dean added.

Erin rolled his words around in her head for several moments, considering her answer carefully.

"Do you want the truth?" Erin asked.

"I do," Dean replied.

"My father is the alleged evil sea captain that murdered all those women. I'm not going for the elixir Dean, I'm going to find my father," Erin replied.

"How do you know that he was your father?" Dean asked.

"In my dream, I can hear my name being called, telling me to come to this magic cave, set back deep within the jungle. Every time I make it to the cave, the voice calls out to me, asking me to save him. I always ask the voice who they are and it replies the same, saying that they're my father. Then I get vivid images of the past. I can see The Crow Men and the captain but the outcome is different than the legend states. Instead, The Crow Men were naturally evil people, and enslaved the sea captain, claiming and torturing his soul for eternity," Erin replied.

"If he is in fact my father, then I need to save him," Erin added.

"But The Crow Men flayed him alive, cursing him and the island for the rest of time," Dean said confused.

"According to the legend, yes. But I don't believe in the legend. I believe in what I've been shown and I refuse to believe my father would harm anyone," Erin replied.

"What do ye hope to gain from finding him?" Dean asked her.

"I want the truth about my history. Why he gave me up, who he was, and why I wasn't worth keeping. I also want to know what he was doing on that island in the first place. I want the truth," Erin said honestly.

Dean watched Erin closely, looking deep into her eyes but all he could see was a raw pain looking back at him.

"Why is the past so important to you, lass?" Dean asked her.

"I want to know where I come from and what my life could have been like had I not been discarded away like an old forgotten toy," Erin responded.

"What about your crew?" Dean asked.

"No one but you knows my true motives for finding the island and I intend to keep it that way. The crew are like my brothers, yes, but nothing can ever replace the feeling of true family," Erin said.

"What if you don't find what you're looking for, lass?" Dean asked.

"Then I suppose I can finally move on, never getting the answers I seek," Erin replied sadly.

Dean and Erin sat in silence for some time, as the sun began to sink behind the horizon. The stars filled the night sky, as the moon illuminated The Hollow.

"Better get some rest," Erin said finally.

"Aye, I'll see ya in the morning, lass," Dean replied, standing up from the crate and walking towards the stairs that led below deck.

Erin sat there, staring out into the night sky, wondering about her parents. So many questions filled her mind, but tonight was not the night to receive those answers.

Chapter Three

The sun was rising over the horizon as Erin awoke the next morning. She sat up in her bed and placed her head in her hands, not quite prepared to start the day. Suddenly a knock came at her cabin door.

"Enter," Erin said.

Malakai entered the room in a panic.

"Aye, captain ye are gonna want to see this!" Malakai exclaimed.

Erin immediately jumped out of bed and pulled her leather boots on quickly, grabbing her hat and following Malakai out of the room and up the stairs to the main deck above.

"O'er the horizon captain," Malakai said, pointing out to the vast ocean.

Erin grabbed the spyglass from Malakai and pointed it over towards the horizon where she finally saw it. A black ship with black sails that had the jolly roger embroidered upon them. Captain Blackstone.

There was only one reason he would be this far from Tortuga. He must know about the island and the elixir and have followed them from the port. Erin thought back to her conversation with Dean in the tavern. Is it possible they were overheard? After all, Blackstone's men were all around when they were discussing the journey.

All they could do now was try and outrun Blackstone but Erin knew they wouldn't get far enough. The Bloody Fortune was said to be the fastest ship the Dark Sea had ever seen, outrunning even the most cunning of pirates and sealing their fate in Davey Jones' Locker.

Erin handed the spyglass back to Malakai and stepped up to the helm, as she turned it sharply to the right, steering The Hollow away from Blackstone, leading the chase. The Bloody Fortune followed suit, cutting through the waves like a knife. It was fast, too fast for The Hollow as Blackstone started closing in on them, leaving no room for escape. Erin knew they were going to have to fight their way out of this or die trying.

Suddenly, The Hollow shook with a malevolent force and everything was tossed sideways, including Erin and Dean. The ship rocked again with an angry force as Erin yelled out, "Batten down the hatches and prepare to fight boys! Blackstone is upon us!"

The sound of swords being unsheathed was thunderous as the crew prepared to fight. The Bloody Fortune ran into the side of The Hollow once more, sweeping across the side and sitting parallel to it on the briny deep. Battle cries filled the air as Blackstone's crew started swinging over on the ropes of the sail to board The Hollow when Erin yelled, "Kill them all!"

The fighting ensued, as she grabbed for her sword. The sound of clanging was loud as she watched her crew fight bravely. The roar of screams was unbearable as bodies were falling left and right, blood splattering across the deck. Erin could sense someone come up behind her so she swung her sword to meet theirs; it was Blackstone.

"So ye think ye can steal the elixir from me, lass?" Blackstone asked.

"It's not stealing if it never belonged to you in the first place!" Erin exclaimed.

"Oh, but it is mine. Everything the Dark Sea touches is my property. Now ye will suffer the consequences!" He exclaimed.

As their swords were still merged, Erin leaned back and kicked at Blackstone's chest, sending him backward. He landed with a 'thud' and looked at her with such rage in his cold, black eyes. Just as quick as he went down, he got up and came after her, swords clanging, the fight had just begun.

As they worked their way around the deck, it resembled a dance almost. Swords clashing, both fighting for life. They knew only one of them was going to make it out of this alive and Erin was determined to make sure it was her. As the fight raged on, Blackstone took a step toward Erin and caught her off guard, hitting her in the face with the back of his hand.

"Ye made a big mistake trying to take me on," Blackstone said.

"I will beat you," Erin stated through gritted teeth.

As she spun around and swung her sword, she caught Blackstone across the face. Blood dripped down his cheek, which made him appear even more menacing.

"Nice shot lass, but it'll be ye last!" He yelled.

Blackstone lunged at Erin and missed, as their swords met and looped around. Swords swinging, Blackstone lunged again but this time caught Erin in the right shoulder. A sharp pain radiated through her arm as her snow-white shirt turned crimson. She let out a soul-piercing scream as she fell to her knees, dropping her sword at his feet. Blackstone stood tall over Erin as she tried to nurse her injured shoulder.

"Any last words lass?" He asked her, placing his sword against Erin's throat.

"I should be asking you that," She replied.

Blackstone hesitated for just a moment, long enough for Dean to jam his sword upward into Blackstone's heart from behind.

Blackstone fell to the deck, blood pooling out around his lifeless body. Suddenly the sound of swords falling radiated throughout the ship. His crew had surrendered. After all, the crew falls with the captain as tradition goes.

"Unless you want to meet your captain's fate, I suggest ye get off my ship! NOW!" Erin exclaimed as Blackstone's men started to run to the side and jump overboard while others swung back on the ropes across the briny deep to The Bloody Fortune.

"Throw his body overboard. Let the Kraken have at him!" Erin yelled.

As Erin walked away from Blackstone's body, she started going around the deck to count how many of her men they had killed. Bodies lay lifeless all over the ship, blood coating the once brown wood. A little less than half of her crew of twenty was gone. The rest of the bodies were part of Blackstone's crew. The guilt set in and weighed heavy on her heart. Her men were only in this situation because of Erin.

As she heard a 'splash' come from behind her, she knew that Blackstone forever belonged to the Dark Sea now.

Erin climbed up to the helm, commanding the attention of her remaining crewmates.

"You fought bravely for me maties, but many of our comrades have lost their lives on this day. Prepare them for burial and take the utmost care. These men were our family, our friends, and our protectors. It's the least we can do for them now" Erin announced.

The crew could see how broken and guilty Erin felt over losing her men but they didn't say anything. They simply nodded and started to round up the bodies of their fallen while the bodies of their enemies were tossed overboard like garbage. Erin slowly made her way across the deck to the stairs and started to descend them, making her way to her cabin. Upon entering the room, blood started to drip from her hand onto the floor, her shirt completely stained crimson as she was losing a lot of blood.

"Erin, you need to sit down," Dean called from behind her.

"I can't. These men, my men, they died because of me," Erin said sobbing.

Dean wrapped his arms around Erin and held her tightly as she wept into his chest.

"No Erin, they died for you! There's a difference. They loved you and would have done anything for you. That's what family does" Dean said.

"Then why do I feel so guilty?" Erin asked him.

"Because you loved them and now, they're gone. But it's not your fault" He replied, holding Erin closer.

"They knew that your adventure to the island came with some risk," Dean added.

"I loved them." That statement had never been uttered before. She didn't even know what love was as she never experienced it before, yet something ached deep in her chest. Is this what love and heartache felt like? Because maybe she was never as empty and alone as she thought. Her men laid their lives down for her. That was the most courageous thing anyone had ever done for her before. She did love them; they were her brothers and now they were gone. But she would ensure they would never be forgotten.

Dean grabbed Erin and pulled her over to the bed.

"Sit down while I clean your wound," He said.

Erin took a seat as she started to unbutton her once-white shirt. Dean stopped for a moment and took in her beauty, the way her breasts curved, and the smoothness of her porcelain skin. He couldn't believe just how breathtaking she was.

Dean walked back towards Erin, holding a bottle of rum in one hand and an old shirt in the other. He ripped the shirt into multiple shreds and proceeded to open the rum.

"This is going to hurt," He said.

"Just do it," Erin said through gritted teeth.

Dean took the bottle of rum and poured it over her shoulder. Erin let out a scream as the liquid ran down her arm creating a pool at her feet. Dean took a strip of the old shirt and tied it tightly around Erin's arm to try and control the bleeding. Then he wrapped her shoulder up, tying it off at the end. He studied her for several moments, seeing the pain in her eyes.

"Are you alright?" Dean asked her.

"I'm fine," She lied as she threw on another shirt.

"We're going to have to watch that for infection, lass," He replied.

"I don't care anymore, Dean. I got my men killed, I don't deserve to live," Erin replied sadly.

"Don't say that. You did everything you could to protect them and they knew how much they mattered to you," Dean said.

"Did they? Because I never told them just how much I loved them, and now it's too late," Erin said.

"It's never too late Erin. Come with me," Dean said, holding out his hand for her to take.

Erin placed her hand in his as he escorted her out of the cabin and back up the stairs to the main deck. He led her over to the side of The Hollow and stood behind her, holding her at the waist.

"Tell them now Erin, they're listening," Dean said.

Tears started to fall down her cheeks as she tried to gather the words and strength to say goodbye to her men. Erin peered out over the briny deep, as it glistened in the sunlight, looking over the horizon and imagining each of her lost crewmates.

"I'm so sorry I couldn't save you, you were my family, my friends, my brothers, and I let you down. I was supposed to protect you, but you ended up protecting me. Rest in peace now maties, you will never be forgotten. I love you all," Erin said.

As she looked up, dozens of seagulls flew overhead and Erin felt a calming relief. Her fallen men had heard her and they were there with her, their souls flying free. She could feel an ease radiate through her as she realized her men were not gone; they were still guiding her on her journey and Erin was at peace.

Dean held Erin close as he wrapped his arms around her from behind, resting his head on top of hers.

"I need to tell you something, lass," Dean said.

"What is it?" Erin asked.

"I'm falling in love with you," Dean replied.

Erin was taken by surprise. It was the last thing she ever expected to hear in her life. She paused for a few seconds and formed her words carefully.

"You shouldn't love me, Dean," Erin replied.

"Why do you say that?" He asked her.

"I'm damaged from years of abandonment and abuse. I barely know how to love anyone, let alone what it even means. You don't want me, Dean," Erin said.

"I don't want you lass, I need you. There's a difference," Dean replied.

"I need you like a man needs air to survive, like the waves need the beach, and like the sun needs the moon," Dean added.

Erin took a deep breath and turned around to face him, pulling his face down to hers, and kissing him on the lips. With passion and hunger, Erin and Dean embraced in the kiss for what felt like hours, just holding each other, and melding together into one soul.

Erin was starting to love Dean but she wasn't ready to admit it yet. She needed more time and right now, they had all the time in the world.

Chapter Four

The next morning, the deck had been scrubbed clean and all signs of the fight were erased. Everyone was exhausted as the sun beat down on The Hollow, releasing an unforgiving heat wave. It was humid and the crew was miserable as they all gathered below deck to play a game of dice.

Erin was in her cabin, writing in a leather-bound journal, while Dean was gambling with the crew. Erin used this time alone to gather her thoughts and detail the last few days, making sure she didn't miss a thing. Journaling was the only escape Erin had when they were out at sea. It was where her deepest thoughts, desires, and fears roamed free where no one else could find them.

As Erin continued documenting the journey and her feelings for Dean, a strange ominous feeling suddenly overwhelmed her. Something was wrong but she didn't know what it was. Erin tried to brush the feeling off, but it had a hold of her and she just couldn't shake it.

Just then a knock came at the door.

"Enter," Erin said.

"Hello lass, what are ye doing in here all by yourself?" Dean asked.

Erin quickly closed the journal, wrapping the leather string around it and tying it closed.

"I was documenting the journey since so much has happened the last few days. I'd hate to forget anything," Erin replied.

Dean studied Erin as she concentrated on the journal. He noticed she was acting distant and couldn't figure out why.

"Is something wrong lass?" Dean asked her.

Erin paused for a few moments, considering how best to answer the question.

"I can't shake the feeling that something big is coming, something out of our control," Erin said.

"We're getting closer to the island, of course you're feeling this way. The men that inhabit the island alone are more terrifying than anything else we could encounter," Dean replied.

"Yeah, you're probably right. I just couldn't live if anything else happened to my remaining crewmates," Erin said.

"Nothing is going to happen to them lass, don't fret," Dean replied as he lifted Erin's chin and kissed her deeply.

The passion radiated through them like lightning to metal, evoking such desires that Erin only dreamed about. As Erin stood, Dean wrapped his arms around her body, running his hands down her back. Erin's arms were wrapped around his neck as the heat between them continued to rise. Erin started to walk backward, pulling Dean along with her towards the bed in the corner. Dean laid Erin down gently and proceeded to carefully unbutton her shirt, revealing her breasts. He bent down and started kissing at her neck, moving down to her chest, taking a nipple into his mouth, biting gently.

Erin let out a moan of ecstasy as she lifted Dean's shirt over his head, revealing defined muscles and a profound V. She traced the muscles with her finger as she felt herself grow wet and pulse with need. Dean pulled Erin's leather boots off her feet, then worked his way to her pants, untying them and pulling them off. He ran his hands over her thigh, stopping between her legs where he lowered his mouth and took her in. Dean sucked and licked at Erin, as she bucked on the bed from the pleasure. Just when Erin thought it couldn't get better, Dean inserted two fingers inside of her and wiggled them back and forth until Erin let out a scream.

Erin moaned and yelled out Dean's name as he finally came up for air and peered deep into her eyes.

"Don't stop," Erin begged.

"Oh lass, I'm just getting started," Dean replied with that handsome grin on his face.

He kissed her with a hunger and a force Erin never felt before as if their souls were merging into one with every touch. Dean unbuckled his pants and pulled them down just enough. He shoved himself deep inside of Erin, thrusting back and forth as she wrapped her legs around him, running her nails down his back.

"Oh Dean," Erin moaned.

"Harder."

Dean obliged her request. It was as if they couldn't get enough, as Erin pulled Dean down for a kiss. He continued to thrust steadily as he bit her bottom lip, teasing at it with his tongue.

"I'm almost there, lass," Dean said.

"Me too," Erin replied.

"Just a little more."

Dean increased his pace as Erin's eyes rolled into the back of her head. Her back arched, lifting off of the bed as they moaned together in unison. After several moments, Dean started to slow down as Erin's body shook from the ecstasy. As Dean stopped, he took his right hand and ran it down Erin's cheek, and whispered, "I love you lass."

Erin wasn't ready yet so she simply pulled Dean in for another kiss as he laid down next to her and she adjusted herself, laying her head onto his chest. Dean held Erin so tightly as she wrapped her arm around his waist, their hearts belonging to one another.

As Erin laid on Dean's chest, she asked him, "What are your plans for after we find the island?"

"What do you mean, lass?" Dean asked.

"What things do you want to do in your life?" Erin asked.

Dean considered her question carefully with a smile upon his face.

"Well, lass I would like to find a nice plot of land to build a proper home upon it for you and me. I want to show you what 'home' means and how great love can be. I see us having children and teaching them the ways of the briny deep, passing on the legends and adventures you've encountered. There's nothing left for me to do or see in this world, because I have everything I need right here in my arms," Dean replied.

Erin smiled and looked up at Dean.

"It sounds simply perfect," Erin said.

"How many children so you see us having?" She asked.

"Two boys, and a girl, as strong and as determined as you are," Dean said.

Erin never thought of building a life before, let alone with someone else. The thought of having a place to call her own scared her, but also excited her with all the possibilities. Especially children. She never saw herself as a mother before but picturing a daughter that took after her, made her happy. She would ensure any children they had, would not grow up the way she did, never knowing love or acceptance. It was a vow she swore to herself in that very moment.

"You're going to be a great father," Erin said.

"And you're going to be an even better mother," Dean replied as he kissed the top of her head.

*　　*　　*　　*　　*

As the day drifted into night, Erin was startled out of her slumber.

"Do you hear that?" Erin asked, waking Dean up from a dead sleep.

Erin rolled over and looked around the cabin but couldn't see anything. However, a haunting melody could be heard throughout the ship, so beautiful and captivating.

"Where is that music coming from?" Erin asked, confused.

"I'm not sure lass," Dean replied.

Dean and Erin climbed out of bed, quickly throwing on their clothes and boots. Together they walked over to the door, opening it slowly, peering out into the deserted hall. The music grew louder as they walked towards the stairs that led up to the main deck. Dean walked ahead of Erin, prepared to protect her should anything be awry. As they hit the top step, the warm night air was perfumed by the smell of flowers. It was humid but the air was still and the briny deep was calm. They walked hand in hand to the helm and peered out over the ship but it was empty; not a soul in sight. The music continued its melody when finally, they saw it. Out in the water were hundreds of sirens swimming circles around the ship. They looked like sharks circling their prey right before an attack, and fear struck Erin right in the heart.

"We must be in Widow's Crossing," Erin said.

Suddenly, the ship was rocked by a turbulent force, sending Dean and Erin flying across the deck. The sirens were bombarding the ship, trying to sink it. As protectors of the sea, they were obligated to stop trespassers from finding The Island of the Immortals, at all costs.

"We're under attack!" Erin screamed.

As quickly as Erin shouted out, her crew came running from below deck.

"Mann your station's maties and keep your eyes peeled, these are dangerous creatures," Erin commanded.

The tales of sirens were centuries old. As protectors of the island, they would sing out to traveling sailors to try and intoxicate them with their songs in the hopes they would kill themselves. The ones who could resist the siren's song were torn from limb to limb instead. Many ships were sunk by the sirens and thousands of lives were lost. They protected the Dark Sea from trespassers heading towards the lost island, which meant there was something there worth protecting.

Again, the ship was rocked with such a force, that it sent the crew tumbling sideways.

"Batten down the hatches mates, we're in for a rough ride!" Erin exclaimed.

Erin ran to the helm and took control of The Hollow, sharply turning her to the right. She knew they couldn't win against the sirens if it came down to a fight, so she had to get them out of there instead. Erin whipped the helm back and forth, trying to overpower the hits the ship was taking. She knew if she didn't get them out of there, they were all going to be sleeping deep in Davey Jones' Locker.

The song grew louder as Erin looked over and saw Sebastian and Malakai, each with knives to their throats.

"NO! STOP!" She screamed.

But it was too late. The sirens had them deep in a trance and Sebastian and Malakai slit their throats. Erin screamed out in pain, unable to stop the siren's song. Malakai and Sebastian's bodies hit the deck, blood pooling everywhere as the ship continued to take powerful hits from the circling sirens.

"Everyone get below deck; you'll be safer there!" Erin commanded.

"No! We are not leaving you!" Dean cried.

"I am the captain of this ship and I just gave you all a direct order!" Erin stated.

"Now go!"

Dean and the crew turned and ran to the stairs that led below deck. Erin couldn't chance anymore of her men succumbing to the siren's song. She was determined to not lose anyone else so she grabbed the helm and spun it to the left, cutting through the circle of sirens below.

Erin maneuvered The Hollow as fast as she could, to try and get out of Widow's Crossing alive. The sky above started to turn a pale pinkish-orange and Erin knew the sun would be their saving grace, she just had to hold on a little longer.

Another hit violently rocked the ship and Erin feared they were going to take on water and capsize. She was steering The Hollow away as fast as possible but Erin worried it wouldn't be enough. As the sun started to rise over the horizon and the sunlight illuminated the sky, the siren's song stopped and the air was quiet and still. The Hollow stopped rocking and everything was calm again.

Erin let out a sigh of relief as thunderous footsteps could be heard running up the stairs and over towards Erin.

"What happened?" Dean asked.

"Sirens don't like the sunlight," Erin confirmed as she peered out over the Dark Sea and no longer saw any sign of the sirens. They were safe, for now.

Erin looked out at her men, seeing the fear still stricken in their eyes.

"Men, check the ship for damages and see what you can do to repair it until we make land. I'll handle our fallen crewmates," Erin said.

The crew dispersed and did as they were told as Erin and Dean just looked at each other, the fear still present in their eyes. Erin released the helm and took a deep breath, exhaling slowly.

"Will you help me with Malakai and Sebastian?" Erin asked him.

"Of course, lass. They were fine men," Dean replied.

Erin walked over to the bodies as Dean followed closely behind her. Erin knelt and closed their eyes, taking each of their hands in hers. Erin prayed over Malakai and Sebastian, hoping they had found peace. Tears rolled down her cheek as she just knelt there and wept for her brothers.

"If I knew what this journey entailed, I never would have embarked on it. Please forgive me, brothers," Erin said.

Dean handed Erin some sheets and helped her wrap the bodies in them tightly.

"The rest of the crew needs to say their farewells," Erin said.

Dean understood and went to gather the rest of the crew. When they returned to Erin, they confirmed that the damage to The Hollow was minimal and they would make it to the island.

"Thank you, brothers. Now we must say goodbye to two of our own. Please take a moment and say a prayer for Malakai and Sebastian, two of the best and most loyal crewmates the Dark Sea has ever seen," Erin announced.

The crew gathered around the bodies of their fallen brothers and embraced hands, saying a silent prayer for them. Once they said their farewells, Dean and the crew tossed the bodies overboard into the briny deep.

"The sirens got close to us and took our men, but I'm afraid the fight isn't over," Erin said.

"What do ye mean, lass?" Dean asked.

"The sirens only stopped attacking because of the sunlight, which means they'll attack again tonight. We are in their territory and they are trying to keep us away from the island at all costs.," Erin replied.

"Then we'll be ready for them," Dean said as the crew cheered in agreement.

Chapter Five

The day was long and hot as the sun above beat down brutally on The Hollow. Erin and the crew spent the day reinforcing the ship and battening down the hatches. She knew the sirens would return tonight and they all had to be prepared. They got off easy the night before but she had a sinking feeling that they wouldn't be so forgiving tonight.

As the sun sank further and further below the horizon, Erin couldn't help but count down the hours until the attack. She had a knife strapped to her thigh, one in her boot, and her sword sheathed to her hip. She was as ready as she was going to be.

The crew was gathered on the main deck playing cards as Erin paced back and forth from the helm to the side of the ship, peering over the edge from time to time but there was no sign of the sirens yet. Dean tried his best to soothe

Erin's anxiety and would rub her back but Erin would just pull away. She was lost in thought, concentrating on something, but Dean wasn't sure what it was.

Erin stopped pacing and turned to Dean finally.

"Come with me," She said.

"Where are we going, lass?" Dean asked.

Erin simply rose on her tiptoes and kissed Dean, grabbing his hand. As she pulled away, she started towards the stairs that led below deck with Dean following in tow. As they descended the stairs and entered Erin's cabin, Dean was slightly aware that something was wrong but Erin turned towards him, kissing him so deeply that he completely forgot everything else.

"Close your eyes," Erin said as she pulled away from Dean.

Dean looked at her longingly, taking his hand and brushing her cheek. Finally, Dean closed his eyes and stood alone in the middle of the room as Erin walked quickly towards the door.

"Please forgive me," Erin said as she closed the door behind her, locking it tightly.

Dean ran towards the door and tried to pull it open but it wouldn't budge.

"Erin! Erin, don't do this," He shouted.

"It's the only way to keep you safe," Erin replied as she walked towards the stairs and headed towards the main deck.

Dean pounded on the door, yelling for someone, anyone to hear him and let him out but it was no use. No one could hear his cries. Dean was in a panic, unable to do anything while everyone was above deck, preparing to fight the sirens. How could Erin do this to him? She knew he could hold his own.

Questions swirled through Dean's mind as he continued to pound on the door, knowing it was no use. He looked around the cabin for any way out, but there was nothing. He was trapped.

Above deck, Erin gathered her crew together, aware that morale was low.

"Avast ye maties, evil is coming and we must be ready. The melody they sing is intoxicating, you must resist it with all your strength. Stay away from the sides of the ship and stick to the helm. If we are to win this fight, we must remain together. We are family and we are fighting for one another, so let's show them hell!" Erin exclaimed.

A cry erupted from the crew as they held their swords up in the air, prepared to fight. Just as everyone gathered around the helm, the ship jerked and groaned.

"Stand your ground" Erin exclaimed.

Swords at the ready, the men peered around, watching, and waiting.

The melodic tune was beautiful as it filled the night air, making the hair on the back of Erin's neck stand on end. The men started to lower their swords as the melody encased them.

"Swords at the ready!" Erin exclaimed, breaking through the trance the men were under.

The crew shook their heads and tried to focus, even though the haunting song was intoxicating. Again, the ship jerked, rocking to the side with such a malevolent force. The sirens were circling the ship, preparing to make their move.

A dense fog surrounded The Hollow, thicker than anything Erin had ever encountered before. She could barely see 3 feet in front of her as she called out to her men.

"Stay together mates and be prepared for anything," Erin stated.

The ship was rocking back and forth across the briny deep with a force so strong, that Erin worried they might capsize. Screeching came from the Dark Sea below, as dozens of sirens started to climb up the sides of the ship. Erin was scared because sirens aren't supposed to have legs, only tails, yet here they were, mounting The Hollow. As they started to climb aboard, several sang their intoxicating tune as others screeched and hissed at the crew.

They had made their way on board the ship and there was no turning back.

The lead siren locked eyes with Erin, standing up off the edge of the ship and making its way towards her. Erin grabbed for her blade off her thigh and angled it out, facing the siren. The siren stopped moving toward Erin and everything fell silent for a moment until the leader let out a screeching hiss, that echoed throughout the ship.

The siren resumed walking towards Erin as its grey scaley face oozed puss and featured numerous scars. Its hair was missing chunks and the rest was caked to its grey and damaged skin. Erin lunged out at the siren as it closed in on her, slashing the blade in the air. The siren moved with such ease, that it avoided contact with the blade entirely.

Erin could hear yelling coming from behind her. She turned quickly to see her crew fighting the sirens, trying to stop them from pushing their way toward Erin. That's when she realized it wasn't the crew they wanted, it was her.

Erin felt something grab at her injured shoulder, so she threw her arm out, shoving the blade deep into the siren's chest. It let out a piercing scream and stumbled back a few steps as it pulled the blade out, throwing it to the ground but there was no blood as the siren continued towards Erin as if nothing had happened.

They did everything in their power to try and slow the sirens down, but it was no use. The weapons of man were useless against the sirens.

Suddenly a 'bang' came from below deck. Dean.

Dean had thrown himself against the door to try and open it, finally mustering enough strength to break through. Erin knew instantly what that sound was as she could see Dean running up the stairs to the main deck.

"Lass!" Dean shouted.

"Stay back Dean," Erin replied.

Erin unsheathed her sword, twirled around, and swung out at the sirens, cutting them in the stomach. But again, it did not harm them. Whatever the sirens were made of, they were immune to her weapons.

The siren closest to Erin reached out for her, grabbing her by the throat as Dean came running up from behind, tossing the siren to the ground.

"Erin, we have to get out of here," He cried.

"There's nowhere to go. They don't want the crew Dean, they want me!" She exclaimed.

Dean looked around and noticed the crew was pushing back at the sirens, keeping them away from Erin as much as they could. Why did they only want Erin? As he was distracted, the siren picked Dean up and threw him up against the helm, knocking him unconscious.

"Noooo!" Erin cried out running to Dean and checking his pulse.

He was breathing. Erin felt a wave of relief for just a moment as the fear returned, eating away at her. Erin racked her brain for a way out of this mess but the only way she could think of to protect Dean and her crew was to give herself up to the sirens.

"Fine, take me just don't harm my men!" Erin exclaimed.

The chaos ceased as the lead siren held her grey and mutated hand out for Erin to take.

Erin knelt next to Dean and kissed him, whispering in his ear, "I love you" before she stood up and placed her hand in the sirens.

As Erin neared the side of the ship, she turned to face her crew, their faces struck with pure fear and disbelief. They had sailed with Erin for ten years; they were her crew of misfits. How could they go on without their captain and friend?

"You have all fought valiantly for me, but now it's my turn to fight for you. I love you all," Erin said as tears started to fall down her cheek, landing on the siren's hand.

The siren let out a soul-piercing scream of pain as Erin clapped her hands to her ears, blood trickling over her hands. The sirens turned and jumped overboard back into the briny deep, leaving Erin to fall to her knees from the

ng pain. Her heart began to race and her breath
ee ragged as everything slowly started to fade from her
vision, eventually going black.

"Erin, slow down," Troy shouted as he chased behind her.

"Come on ya slowpoke," Erin called out with a chuckle.

"Are we almost there?" Troy asked her.

Erin came to an abrupt stop, causing Troy to run into her.

"What did you go and do that for?" Troy asked, rubbing his head.

"Shhh," Erin whispered as she knelt behind some barrels, pulling Troy with her.

Together they listened as a familiar sea shanty filled the air.

'Yo ho, yo ho, a pirate's life for me!' mysterious voices sang.

Erin had been watching this group of misfits for weeks. They would play cards and gamble, tell stories of their adventures and muddled childhoods, and talk about finding a captain one day so they could once again sail the Dark Sea.

"It's them, they're perfect!" Erin exclaimed to Troy.

"Perfect for what?" Troy asked confused.

"To be my crew," Erin said confidently.

"They're looking for a captain Troy," Erin said.

"What makes you think they'll sail with you?" Troy asked.

"I have The Hollow," Erin replied, smiling.

The group of misfits had long been sailing the Dark Sea together until they lost their captain during a storm.

They could've joined another pirate's crew but they weren't looking for just anyone. They wanted a special captain, someone worthy of sailing with. Erin knew that she could relate to the men because their childhoods were similar. Orphanages to self-made men, all without taking a handout. They knew hard work and sacrifice and Erin knew they were the crew she wanted behind her.

"Oi, who are ya?" A voice asked from behind Erin and Troy, causing the rest of the group to stop singing and look over at the commotion.

Erin looked up to see one of the misfits looking down at her and Troy, confused.

"I'm Erin and I'm here to ask you all to be my crew," Erin said confidently.

The men simply laughed at her remark.

"And what makes ye think you're worthy of our loyalty?" The man asked.

"I have a ship, I have gold, and I have an adventure for us to embark upon," Erin replied.

"How'd a young lass such as yourself get a ship with gold?" He asked her.

"I stole the gold and purchased the ship," Erin said honestly.

The men looked from one another and then back at Erin.

"Why do you want us?" He asked.

"I know what it feels like to grow up without a family, without love, and to always be on your own. I think we can help each other. You want to sail the Dark Sea and I need a crew," Erin said.

The men simply looked around at each other and after several moments nodded in agreement.

"Aye, you've got yourself a crew lass!" The man exclaimed.

"What's your name?" Erin asked as she stuck out her hand for him to shake.

"It's Malakai. Malakai Parker," He replied, shaking her hand.

Chapter Six

Erin woke the next morning in her bed, not knowing how she got there. She tried to recall the events from the night before but it was all a blur. All she could remember was the pain and the blood dripping out of her ears. Quickly, she looked at her hands but they were clean, with no blood in sight.

Dean appeared in the doorway, leaning against the side, watching Erin.

"How are ya feeling this morning lass? Ya gave us quite the fright," He asked.

"What...what happened?" Erin asked, confused.

"What do you remember?" Dean asked her.

"The sirens climbed aboard the ship and were trying to get to me. The crew tried to stop them but the sirens were immune to our weapons. I wanted to prevent any more death so I agreed to go with them. That's when it gets hazy," Erin said.

"You made the ultimate sacrifice by trading your life for the crew. That kind of selfless act of love must be something the sirens can't fight against because your tears touched the siren's skin and she screeched, fleeing back to the Dark Sea taking the others with her," Dean replied.

"The blood and the pain…" Erin trailed off.

"Sirens are selfish creatures, banished to the Dark Sea by the Sea Hag centuries ago. Their screech is enough to kill someone, popping all their blood vessels with one yell, but you survived," Dean said.

Dean walked over to Erin and sat down on the bed next to her.

"I just don't understand why they would want me," Erin said.

"They must have recognized something within you, whether it be pain or longing, but they must have wanted to claim you as one of their own," Dean replied.

"You did a brave thing, lass," Dean added.

"I would do anything to protect my crew. I would do anything to protect you," Erin said as she looked into Dean's eyes.

Dean ran his fingers down her cheek, stopping to tuck the fallen hair behind Erin's ear.

"Dean…I need you to know just how much I love you," Erin replied.

"Did you just say what I think you did?" Dean asked amused.

"I did and I do," Erin said with a smile.

"I love you too, Erin," Dean said as he kissed her.

The entire world drifted away at that moment, only leaving Erin and Dean to embrace. Their worries about the sirens and the elixir, all disappeared. Nothing else mattered more than their love and now Erin was finally able to admit it out loud.

As if they were floating, Dean and Erin kissed so passionately, so deeply, as if it was the last kiss they'd ever have. Finally, Dean pulled away, holding her face in his hands.

"We need to get you back in ship shape, lass. We'll be arriving at the island by tonight!" Dean stated.

"Tonight? Are you sure?" Erin asked.

"Yes, I've been studying the maps and tracking our movement through the Dark Sea. We should be able to see The Island of the Immortals just after sunset," Dean said.

Erin hesitated for a moment and then asked Dean, "Are you still wanting to go there to die?"

Dean could sense the panic and fear behind Erin's question. After all the years of abandonment, it made perfect sense.

"No lass, that's not what I want anymore. Things changed the moment I set eyes on you in that tavern and I knew I had to make you mine," Dean replied.

"I was so cruel to you, why would you want me then?" Erin asked him.

"There was just something about ya. You were different than any other woman I've ever met. I loved Sarah and Annie, they were my entire world, but you taught me to embrace new opportunities. I believe they have found peace and that puts me at ease, but I believe you to be my soulmate Erin," Dean said.

Erin could feel the sincerity wash over her as Dean looked deep into her eyes and she knew it was true. Dean was her soulmate, everything she had ever been searching for when it came to love, without even looking for it.

Chapter Seven

A few hours later, Erin joined the crew out on the main deck as she noticed something in the distance. She grabbed the spyglass from her belt and peered out over the Dark Sea.

"Land ho!" Erin shouted as she pointed towards the East.

"Prepare to make port! Drop the anchor men," Erin commanded.

The crew scrambled around, following her orders to drop the anchor. The Hollow began to slow down, eventually coming to a complete halt.

"Finish gathering the supplies we need and get to the row boats maties!" Erin exclaimed.

Once the boats were loaded, Erin and her crew mates climbed down the ladder into the waiting row boats.

Dean was the last one to climb down the ladder and into a boat.

"Everything alright?" Erin asked him.

"Yes, just had to grab something," Dean replied.

They were one mile from the island, everyone rowing as fast as they could across the Dark Sea. Half an hour passed and the sun was moving lower towards the horizon. Erin knew they needed to get to the island while they still had sunlight.

Finally, as they closely approached the island, everyone climbed out of the row boats and jumped into the briny deep, leading the boats to land by hand. Once on the beach, the crew tied the boats to a nearby rock and Erin checked around to make sure everyone had made it safely.

"Is everyone alright?" Erin asked.

"Aye Aye captain," The crew responded.

Content that they had successfully and safely made it to the island, Erin started to walk inland a bit. Birds could be heard chirping and singing throughout the various trees, while the sound of monkeys chattering away echoed in the distance. Wherever they were, it was unlike any place any of them had ever seen before. It was humid on the island, a drastic temperature change from being out on the briny deep, and the sunlight reflected brightly, shimmering off the crashing waves. The jungle was dense and crustaceans littered the beach along with colorful seashells, making the beach seem otherworldly.

Erin was fascinated with the outer beauty of the island. It was clear this was a place unlike any other as everyone stood on the beach, taking in the magnificence of it all. Erin turned around to face the crew and decided it was best to split everyone up to cover more ground faster,

Erin made two groups. Dean led one and Erin the other.

"Alright lads, the goal is to find the elixir. If we find it, we can sell it to the highest bidder and be set for the rest of our days," Erin said.

A cheer erupted from the crew as they gleefully agreed. Erin pulled the knife from her boot and cut an X into the nearest tree. We'll meet back here in two hours and then head back to The Hollow together," Erin said.

"Dean, do you have a compass?" Erin asked him.

"I sure do, lass," Dean replied.

"Ok lads, be careful out there and don't be late," Erin said.

Dean and his group started walking North, attempting to navigate the thick trees and brush as Erin and her group went South. The crew thought the point of finding the elixir was to sell it and be shrouded in riches, but Erin was here on the island to locate her father, only Dean knowing the truth.

Forty-five minutes passed and there was no water in sight. Erin considered giving up and having the crew turn back since they were all thirsty and exhausted from trekking through the thick jungle. That's when she saw it out of the corner of her eye, a grove of palm trees. Palm trees meant coconuts and coconuts meant water.

"Avast maties, over there!" Erin exclaimed, pointing towards the grove.

Everyone took off running towards the grove, only the faster they ran, the farther away it got. Was she hallucinating? Or was she delirious from lack of fresh water? After running for what felt like miles, they stopped to catch their breath when Erin heard a voice whisper from behind her.

"Come here, Erin."

Erin turned around sharply only there was nothing and no one there. She looked back towards her crew, only they were gone. It was dead silent, only the breeze blowing through the trees could be heard and the distant bird singing in the distance. Where did they go?

Panicked, Erin searched the immediate area, calling out for her men, only to go unanswered. After circling the area for what felt like years, she finally collapsed on the ground from exhaustion.

"Come here, Erin."

Confused and disoriented, Erin stood up and tried to pull her compass out of her pocket. The dial was spinning in circles, there was no way to know the direction where she had come from.

"Walk towards me, Erin."

Erin turned in a circle, looking for the owner of the voice but again, no one was there. Something was wrong and she knew she had to get out of there, quick.

She took off, running as fast as her legs would take her, going deeper into the jungle. Erin ran for as long as she could when suddenly she tripped on a loose vine and landed face-first on the ground.

Pain shot through her injured shoulder causing her to cry out.

"Stop it! Whatever you are, just stop!"

Erin started to realize she may never make it off the island alive. She was just about to give up when she looked up and saw a cave covered in vines and shrubs, illuminated by the sunlight that broke through the jungle canopy. Erin forced herself up and started to walk towards it. She half expected it to be just another hallucination, but as she got closer, so did the cave.

As she grew closer the sound of running water was clear as day. She made it to the entrance of the cave and peered inside. It was lit up with magnificent vivid colors, and the temperature was dramatically different from the outside. It was freezing and Erin began to shiver running her hands up and down her arms.

The inside of the cave glistened like colorful diamonds and as she walked deeper inside, she saw the pool of water rushing down from the base of a waterfall. It was beautiful and so intoxicating, Erin ran to the water and dipped her hands in it, scooping up a handful and taking a sip.

The cool water dripped from Erin's mouth as she took another handful and drank it down. Immediately a calm washed over her, erasing any trace of fear or anxiety that she was feeling. As Erin took another sip of water, the mysterious voice came from behind her.

"Erin, turn around Erin," The voice whispered.

Erin turned around quickly, expecting to find nothing there but instead, there was a white figure of a man standing before her. He was ghostly translucent, simply floating a few inches above the ground.

Erin just stared in awe as she recognized the man standing in front of her. It was the same man described in all the legends about the island.

"Dad?" Erin asked.

"You shouldn't be here Erin, it's too dangerous for you and your crew," Nicholas said.

"Why are you here? How can I see you right now?" Erin asked.

"All those years ago when I was shipwrecked at sea, I found my way to this island for shelter and comfort, only to be greeted by some of the most terrifying men I had ever met. They took me hostage and tied me up. I was unable to move, unable to talk, all I could do was play the memories of you over and over in my mind, but eventually, death found me," Nicholas replied.

"But you're standing right in front of me!" Erin cried.

"I am but a spirit, trapped on this island for eternity, never to move on, never to find peace. The same fate will await you if you don't turn around and leave now," Nicholas said.

"I have so many questions for you," Erin said sadly.

"I know my sweet but we don't have the time," He replied.

"Then make the time!" Erin exclaimed in frustration.

Nicholas sighed and said, "I never abandoned you, Erin. I was sailing to Peril Cove the night I was shipwrecked because I received word that you were born and all I wanted was to get home to you but the storm was too much and it capsized the ship, killing all of my men. I drifted at sea for days until I landed at the shore of this island. At that point, your mother had given you up and I couldn't escape the island. I'm sorry I failed you, Erin."

"Why would The Crow Men take you captive?" Erin asked.

A faint smirk crossed Nicholas' face so quickly Erin thought she imagined it.

"They're an evil people Erin, killing anyone that dare trespass on their land. I was just an unlucky soul to have landed here," Nicholas replied.

"How can I see you?" Erin asked.

"It's the magic of this cave. You can see the ghosts of loved ones who have passed in here. It's how The Crow Men spoke to their ancestors and now it's how you can be here with me," Nicholas said.

"You must be going now my sweet, it won't be long before The Crow Men find you," He added.

Ignoring his warning, Erin looked up at her father and he smiled down at her.

"How can I help you move on?" Erin asked.

"With the elixir. It'll restore me to human form and I can come back. We could be a real family. I'm so sorry you had to grow up without me. I can't imagine the pain you have experienced because of it," He replied.

Nicholas' eyes sparkled with the mention of the elixir. Erin paused for a moment, mulling over her father's words.

Nicholas was lying and she could feel it in her bones.

"What was my mother's name?" Erin asked.

"…Virginia," Nicholas answered.

"No, my mother's name was Charlotte. She was a well-known prostitute in Peril Cove. So, you're lying to me and I want to know why," Erin demanded.

Nicholas glared at Erin with a hatred so concentrated, that the cave began to shake.

"My, aren't you a smart one, lass," Nicholas replied.

"Why are you lying? Who are you?" Erin asked.

An evil smile crossed Nicholas' face as he simply replied, "I am evil incarnate and you dear, are going to set me free."

Chapter Eight

Fear struck Erin in the heart, but she refused to let it show upon her face. She was going to stand her ground and destroy Nicholas, at all costs.

"So, the legend is true. You murdered all those women after The Crow Men saved you from the Dark Sea," Erin stated.

"I see someone knows their history," Nicholas laughed manically.

"Those foolish men made the biggest mistake when they rescued me. I was only traveling the Dark Sea because I was going to be forced to walk the plank. It was my punishment for all the heinous crimes I had committed in my life. You see, I was somewhat of a notorious killer back in my time. Perhaps you heard of me? The Phantom," Nicholas said.

The Phantom was a famous serial killer in the 18th century, plaguing the port of Tortuga and surrounding areas for years. He raped and murdered women nightly, ultimately claiming 165 lives before he was finally captured. Some say he was hanged from a local tree and left out in the sun to rot for days. Others report he escaped and continued to live his life. Reports could never confirm what truly happened to The Phantom, only that the murders suddenly stopped.

Erin knew the stories well, as The Phantom struck in her town of Peril Cove when she was just a baby. No one ever knew what he looked like or his real name. He truly was a phantom.

"Why would you kill The Crow Men's women?" Erin asked.

"It's just in my nature," Nicholas replied.

Erin started to back away a few paces when Nicholas said, "Tsk tsk tsk, there's no leaving now."

"You'll never get me to help you so there's no use in trying," Erin said.

"Oh, but I think I have something up my sleeve," Nicholas replied.

"You wouldn't want to lose Dean, would you?" He asked.

"How do you know about Dean?" Erin asked him.

"I can see everything that happens on this island and I can tell by the look in your eyes, how much he means to you. And let's not forget about your crew. I can smell the guilt on you for losing so many of them already," Nicholas said.

"Don't you dare hurt them!" Erin exclaimed in fury.

"Then get me the elixir!" He cried.

"I don't know where it is," Erin said.

"Yes, you do. Just follow your instincts," Nicholas replied.

Confused, Erin looked around the cave but didn't see anything that looked like an elixir. Frustrated, she took a deep breath and closed her eyes, concentrating on the sound of the waterfall running.

The waterfall.

Erin walked over toward the pool and climbed inside, the water cool and comforting. As she waded through the water, she came to stand in front of the waterfall, watching the water splash its way down the rocks. Instinctively, Erin knew to reach through the waterfall and that the Elixir of Immortality would be there. She stuck her hand through the water and grabbed something hard and cold, pulling it back towards her body.

She looked down and saw the shimmering glass bottle. It was beautiful, pure snow white with diamonds all around it. The elixir was real and Erin was holding it in her hands.

"Bring it here!" Nicholas commanded.

"Promise me first that nothing will happen to Dean or my crew," Erin replied.

"I promise," Nicholas lied.

Erin started to wade back through the pool to the edge, climbing out of the water. She held the elixir tightly in her right hand as she walked over toward Nicholas and stood in front of his ghostly body. She started to raise her hand, offering the elixir to him when suddenly a familiar voice yelled out from behind her.

"Erin don't do it!"

Erin dropped her hand down and quickly turned to look behind her to find Dean and her crew standing in the cave with her.

"What are you doing here?" Erin asked them.

"I don't know. One minute we were trekking through the jungle looking for you and the next minute we were here," Dean said.

Erin thought back to what Nicholas had said previously about the magic of the cave showing you your loved ones that have passed away.

"No! You promised!" Erin screamed out, turning to face Nicholas.

"It was too late for that lass," Nicholas chuckled.

"They were dead the minute you stepped foot in this cave. No doubt succumbing to the many booby traps around the island, created by The Crow Men," He added.

Erin was furious and heartbroken, with so many emotions flooding her at once.

"You can't be dead!" Erin cried out facing back toward Dean and the crew.

Dean just looked at Erin as sadness filled his eyes. A tear rolled down his cheek, and at that moment, he knew it was true.

"I'm so sorry Erin. I never wanted to leave you, especially not like this," Dean said.

"NO! You're not dead, I refuse to believe that!" Erin yelled as she took a step toward Dean reaching her hand out to grab him. Only her hand didn't connect, it fell through his body instead. Dean watched Erin's hand fall through his arm as if she was merely touching the clouds. Erin took a few steps back and began to sob, wrapping her arms around her stomach. The pain was too much to bear. The only family Erin had ever known was dead and there was nothing she could do to save them.

Erin collapsed to the ground, arms still wrapped around herself as she screamed and sobbed out the pain of her loss. Several moments passed when Erin realized, she still had the elixir. She could give it to Dean and the crew and save their lives.

As if Nicholas knew exactly what Erin was thinking, he suddenly said, "It won't work."

"Why not?" Erin asked.

"The elixir was only made as a failsafe for me. Should I have lived through the years of brutality and torture by The Crow Men, the elixir would have ended that suffering, permanently blocking my soul from ever reincarnating. The Crow Men believed that evil couldn't die, so they made the elixir just in case. But now that I'm dead, stuck in this purgatory hell, it will have the opposite effect, bringing me back to form and giving me eternal life. Just

imagine it. The Phantom, the unkillable killing machine,"
Nicholas chuckled.

"Yeah, I like the sound of that," He added.

"If it could save you, it could save them!" Erin
exclaimed.

"Wrong, it would prevent their souls from ever
reincarnating, blocking their passage to eternal peace,"
Nicholas said.

Feeling defeated, Erin let out a soul-piercing scream
that shook the cave floor.

"I will not let you win," Erin replied.

"Oh, but you have no choice lass," Nicholas stated.

Erin knew she had no options. Dean and her brothers
were dead, lost to the dangers of the island. And there was
no way Erin could leave the island knowing The Phantom

was still here, luring others with their dreams, trying to escape his purgatory.

"That's why we received those dreams. You sent them to us?" Erin asked.

"Yes, I knew you'd come. I spent years searching for the perfect victim when one fell into my lap; your father. When he told me he so desperately wanted to get back home to you, I knew I could use it to my advantage," Nicholas replied.

"You made it way too easy, with your abandonment issues and isolation. I could feel your pain, so I tapped into your dreams, leaving false visions and memories behind," He added.

"However, Dean wasn't part of the plan. He intercepted a dream meant for you by mistake. That's the tricky thing about soulmates, they're universally connected," Nicholas said.

"Soulmates?" Erin asked.

"Don't act surprised lass, you've been destined to find him your whole life," Nicholas replied.

"Didn't you ever wonder why your connection was immediately so strong? He ended up just getting in the way of my plan, you were supposed to arrive at the island alone, so I had to leave some traps in place," Nicholas said.

"You evil bastard!" Erin exclaimed.

Nicholas simply let out a laugh, enjoying the pain he was causing Erin.

"If you really killed my father, then tell me, who was he?" Erin asked.

"Edwin Demure. He was traveling the Dark Sea trying to get back to Peril Cove for you. That part wasn't a lie," Nicholas said smugly.

The rage Erin felt intensified. In a matter of a few days, she managed to lose everyone she ever loved as well as the chance to get to know her father. All because of a demented killer with psychic abilities. Erin was fuming and there was nothing she could do to set things right again.

At that moment, she realized she was completely alone in the world, a feeling she used to believe was true when it wasn't. Now those days were gone and she took them for granted. Erin turned to Dean and the crew and whispered, "I love you all, please forgive me."

Uncorking the elixir, Erin sucked it down in one gulp, throwing the empty bottle to the ground as it shattered onto the cave floor. Diamonds and glass flying everywhere.

"NO! You crazy wench! Now you'll never find peace. You'll be stuck here with me for eternity!" Nicholas screamed.

"That's where you have it all wrong," Erin replied smugly.

Erin raised her arms towards the sky, creating an arc, and began to chant in an ancient tongue. Erin didn't know the language but the words freely flowed through her as if she had been speaking it her entire life. A violent wind blew through the cave, causing the vivid colors of the cave to turn black and grey.

"What are you doing?" Nicholas asked in a panic.

"What should have been done years ago," Erin stated.

As Erin continued the chant in the ancient tongue, her eyes glossed over, turning completely white and her back arched as she stood before Nicholas, arms open to the sky. The magic of The Crow Men flowed through Erin as she welcomed the ancestors to use her body as a weapon.

The wind picked up and the cave grew darker.

"Stop! Stop what you're doing and I'll save Dean," Nicholas begged.

"You can't save him! He's already dead," Erin said through gritted teeth.

"I can. I have the ability to bring the dead back to life, you just have to trust me," Nicholas said.

Erin stood there and let the magic of the ancestors fill her veins. She knew that even if Nicholas could bring Dean back, it wouldn't be worth the sacrifice of setting The Phantom free. The realization tore Erin apart inside, knowing she had to say goodbye and let them go.

Erin looked back at Dean and her men and smiled with as much strength as she could muster. They understood what was about to happen as they smiled back at her and Dean mouthed the words 'I love you' in return. Erin closed her eyes as tears fell down her face, squeezing her eyes as tight as they would go. When she opened them again, they were gone.

Erin forced herself to turn back to Nicholas and the rage that fueled her grew even stronger. Adrenaline and magic flowed through her veins as she brought her arms down, holding them out in front of her. A glowing orange light started to flow from her hands; fire.

"You're making a big mistake!" Nicholas cried out.

"No, you made the mistake when you lured me here, now you are going to burn for eternity in Hell," Erin replied.

"You truly are evil; maybe you are my daughter after all," Nicholas said.

Erin watched the fear flash across Nicholas' eyes and a smile radiated across her lips.

"I am the monster you made me."

Erin shot the flames of fire from her hands out at Nicholas, engulfing him. He screamed a blood-curling scream as his body burned alive. The ancestors made sure he was feeling the pain of every one of his victims before letting him succumb to the flames.

Erin put her arms down and just watched Nicholas burn when finally, the screaming stopped and the fire dissipated and all that was left was black ash on the ground.

Satisfied that Nicholas was gone, the ancestors pulled their magic back from Erin, releasing her from their pull. Erin collapsed to her knees, exhausted and full of rage. Erin drew in a few deep breaths and exhaled slowly, trying to regain her balance and strength.

As she pushed herself up from the cave floor, she knew there was no going back to her ordinary life. How could she after everything she had suffered? She was heartbroken and angry and there was only one escape for her.

Erin grabbed the knife that was attached to her thigh. She spun it around in her hands a few times, knowing what she had to do to free herself from this purgatory. Erin took the knife and pointed it toward her chest, pinpointing exactly where her heart was. With all her strength, she pulled the knife out in front of her and after taking a deep breath, she jammed it up into her chest cavity, hitting the center of her heart.

Chapter Nine

Erin hit the ground, blood pooling all around her body. She was lying on her back, looking up, when suddenly the vivid colors and lights returned to illuminate the cave, as beautiful as it had ever been. Erin looked over towards the waterfall and saw Dean, and her crew holding out a hand for her to take. She reached out her arm, trying to reach them but they were too far. Erin closed her eyes and waited to take her final breath.

"Erin…"

Erin opened her eyes at the sound of the voice and saw a beautiful woman with long black hair that framed her delicate face, with eyes that were ocean blue. Brilliant white lights swirled around her, making her appear otherworldly. She knelt down next to Erin and took her hand, holding it tightly.

"Erin, I have a message for you," The woman said.

"Who are you?" Erin asked.

"My name is Natalia, I was the wife of the Chief of The Crow Men and a victim of The Phantom," She said.

"Why...why are you here?" Erin asked weakly.

"I'm here to thank you and offer you a great gift on behalf of my people. You were very brave taking on The Phantom and now my people can finally rest in peace knowing he is gone forever, never to return," Natalia said.

A tear dripped down Erin's cheek and her breathing became weaker as her eyes drifted closed.

"My people and I want to make you protector of our island, Goddess of The Crow Men for you have shown great strength and courage today. These are qualities possessed only by the worthy, and you Erin are worthy," Natalia added.

Natalia took her hand and rested it on Erin's heart. A healing white glow emanated from Natalia's hand and into Erin's chest. Wind swirled around as the colors of the cave danced, the magic encompassing them as Natalia made Erin immortal, breaking the evil curse upon the island.

Erin's wound healed instantly and her breathing returned to normal. Slowly she opened her eyes and looked around but Natalia was gone, as was Dean and her crew. Erin stood up and looked at her reflection in the pool, noticing she was completely transformed. She was wearing a flowing white dress with a flower wreath sitting atop her head. She was the epitome of happiness and beauty.

Erin walked out of the cave and into the brilliant sunlight, soaking in the warmth of its rays. As she stepped out into the jungle, everything changed. The trees became greener, flowers sprouted up from the ground, and a cooling breeze blew through the bluest sky. Everything Erin touched became healthy and beautiful again, breathing life back into the magical island.

With each step Erin took, the ground sprouted grass and the air became pure. The darkness that haunted the island was forever washed away.

As Erin walked back through the jungle to the beach, a familiar voice came from behind her.

"Hello there, lass," Dean said.

Erin turned around quickly to see Natalia, Dean, and her crew.

"How…how are you all here?" Erin asked.

"When you broke the curse, you became the epitome of life itself, restoring all lives lost to the darkness. You saved us all Erin," Natalia said as she waved her arm out to the side revealing her people, The Crow Men.

Women, men, and children all danced around, basking in the joy of the island again.

"You are the Goddess of the Immortals now Erin, Protector of the island and epitome of life itself here on the island. We are all free now that the curse is broken and The Phantom is gone. You gave us our lives back and for that, we are forever grateful," Natalia said.

"I'll leave you now to your family, for you have much to catch up on," Natalia added as she walked away back to her people.

As Erin watched Natalia walk away, Dean came into her view.

"Dean, is that really you?" Erin asked.

"It's really me, lass," Dean replied with a smile across his handsome face.

Erin ran up to Dean and jumped into his arms as he spun her around, kissing her so passionately.

"You're my soulmate Erin and I'll never leave you again. I love you so much," Dean said.

"I love you too Dean, I always will," Erin replied, leaning her head against his.

"Aye, captain, what about us?" The crew asked.

"I did not forget about you boys. You are my brothers, my family, and my protectors and I couldn't have asked for a better bunch of misfits to spend the last ten years with. But I must stay on the island and you maties have things you must do now. So please, take anything you need as The Hollow is yours," Erin said.

Her crew of misfits rushed over and hugged her so tightly.

"We're going to miss you captain," They said.

"And I will miss you all too, but I'll be watching over you, you'll never be alone," Erin replied.

The crew said their final goodbyes and headed for the beach to the row boats that were still tied up on the shore. Erin watched as they rowed out to The Hollow and set sail for their next adventure, wishing them good fortune and safe travels. As The Hollow disappeared over the horizon, she turned to face Dean.

"Will you be staying here with me?" Erin asked him.

"You couldn't get rid of me even if you tried. The Chief of The Crow Men has made me one of them. He felt I was worthy to be an immortal, a protector, and a crow. We can be together for eternity now, lass," Dean replied.

Erin smiled from ear to ear, wrapping her arms around Dean's neck as he held her waist.

"I have something for ya," Dean whispered as he grabbed Erin's left hand and slipped a ring upon it.

"Really?" Erin asked, excitedly.

"Always and forever, lass," Dean replied.

"When did you get this?" Erin asked.

"I bought it in Tortuga, the moment I set eyes on you, I knew we were made for each other," Dean replied.

"But before we can start our lives together lass, there's one more person you need to see," Dean said, turning her to face a man standing up against a palm tree.

"Who is that?" Erin asked.

"Go find out," Dean said as he kissed her briefly before walking away to join The Crow Men in their celebration.

Erin walked over to the man, studying him with every step she took. As she approached him, she asked, "Do I know you?"

"You look just like your mother," Edwin said smiling.

"Dad?" Erin asked confused.

"Yes, it's me Erin," He replied.

"But...how are you here right now? Why?" Erin asked.

"I died on this island Erin, trying to get back home to you. I was lost at sea and found this island that wasn't on any maps, desperate for medical help, food, and water. I wandered into that cave and met Nicholas. He learned about my desperation to get home to my daughter and used that against me. He ended up killing me, taking on my persona to lure you out here to set him free," Edwin said.

"You were coming back for me?" Erin asked.

"When your mother found out she was pregnant, she decided to give the child up upon birth, not wanting to thwart her profession. She never did have a motherly bone in her body but she was beautiful and smart, just like you. I told her I had to go on a mission for a fortnight and once I returned, I would take you and raise you, only I never made it back.

Instead, Charlotte gave you away and you bounced from orphanage to orphanage. Even though I couldn't be there with you, I was always watching over you Erin," Edwin replied.

"Every adventure, every heartbreak, every broken promise in your life, I was there. I watched you grow up into a wise and strong woman, capable of anything. My only regret is that I couldn't give you the life you deserved," Edwin added.

Tears fell down Erin's cheeks as she realized just how much she was wanted and loved. Spending her life searching for these answers, just to find out that supernatural circumstances left her all alone, but now she had been given a second chance. A chance to get to know her father.

"My life may not have been perfect. It's been hard and lonely, but I realized on the journey to this island that I was never truly alone. I had my crew of misfits all along as they were the brothers I never had. Then I met Dean, my soulmate, and now I'm lucky enough to have found you," Erin said as she walked up to Edwin and embraced him in a hug.

"I love you so much Erin," Edwin said.

"I love you too dad," Erin replied.

"Will you be staying on the island with us?" Erin asked him as she pulled away.

"I would love too. I want to get to know my beautiful daughter and the people she protects," Edwin replied.

"Plus, I need to get to know this man that has won your heart," Edwin chuckled.

Erin smiled at Edwin and took him by the hand.

"Plus, you'll need to be here to meet your grandchild," Erin replied.

"A grandchild? Are you sure?" Edwin asked excitedly.

Erin looked down and rubbed her stomach.

"I'm sure. Natalia saved us both," Erin said.

"Does Dean know?" Edwin asked.

"I'm going to tell him tonight after his imitation ceremony," Erin replied.

"Now, come, let's go celebrate," Erin said.

Erin and Edwin joined The Crow Men as everyone gathered around the bon fire and shared stories, folktales, and joyful wishes for their new lives. Dean sat on the other side of Erin and wrapped his arms tightly around her, kissing her on the cheek. The fire raged on into the night, as The Crow Men danced around, celebrating their rebirth and new Goddess.

The peace and magic of the island had finally been restored, as the great Indigenous people of The Island of the Immortals got a second chance. From that day on, they vowed no harm would come to any man that wandered onto their land, as Erin would protect her people, forever maintaining the peaceful and universal balance.

As protector of The Island of the Immortals, she was the purity and love that kept it thriving. Always to watch over it and to guide those who may find their way upon it. The magic and beauty of the island must forever remain intact; a purpose and a gift that Erin accepted graciously.

The End

Made in the USA
Columbia, SC
17 July 2022